Say Hola to Spanish

by Susan Middleton Elya

illustrated by Loretta Lopez

Lee & Low Books Inc. • New York

LEE & LOW BOOKS Inc., 95 Madison Avenue, New York, NY 10016
leeandlow.com

Manufactured in China by South China Printing Co., November 2011

Book design: Christy Hale
Book production: The Kids at Our House
Editorial consultant, Spanish language: Daniel Santacruz

The text is set in Benguiat Frisky, La Bamba, and Marguerita.
The illustrations are rendered in gouache and colored pencil on watercolor paper.

(HC) 15 14 13 12 11 10 9 8
(PB) 20 19 18 17 16 15 14 13 12
First Edition

Library of Congress Cataloging-in-Publication Data
Elya, Susan Middleton.
Say hola to Spanish/by Susan Middleton Elya;
illustrated by Loretta Lopez.
p. cm.
Summary: Introduces Spanish by defining such common words
as "hola" ("hello"), "perro" ("dog"), and "madre" ("mother").
ISBN 978-1-880000-29-8 (hc)   ISBN 978-1-880000-64-9 (pb)
1. Spanish language—Vocabulary—Juvenile literature.
[1. Spanish language—Vocabulary] I. Lopez, Loretta, ill. II. Title.
PC4445.E49 1996
468.1—dc20   95-478   CIP AC

Free Teacher's Guide available
at leeandlow.com

Find out more about Loretta Lopez
at leeandlow.com/booktalk.mhtml

Spanish is fun,

so give it a try.

¡Hola!

Hola is hello,

¡Adiós!

adiós is good-bye.

A dog is a **perro**,
a cat is a **gato**.

You drink from a **vaso**

and eat from a **plato**.

A son is an hijo,

a mother is a madre,

daughter is hija,

and father is padre.

You play in a **parque**,

you live in a **casa**.

Mamá drinks coffee,
café, from a **taza**.

Your hair is your **pelo**,

your nose is **nariz.**

Your grandmother's **pelo**
is probably **gris.**

You sit on a **silla**,

you eat at a **mesa**.

A perfect surprise is called a **sorpresa**.

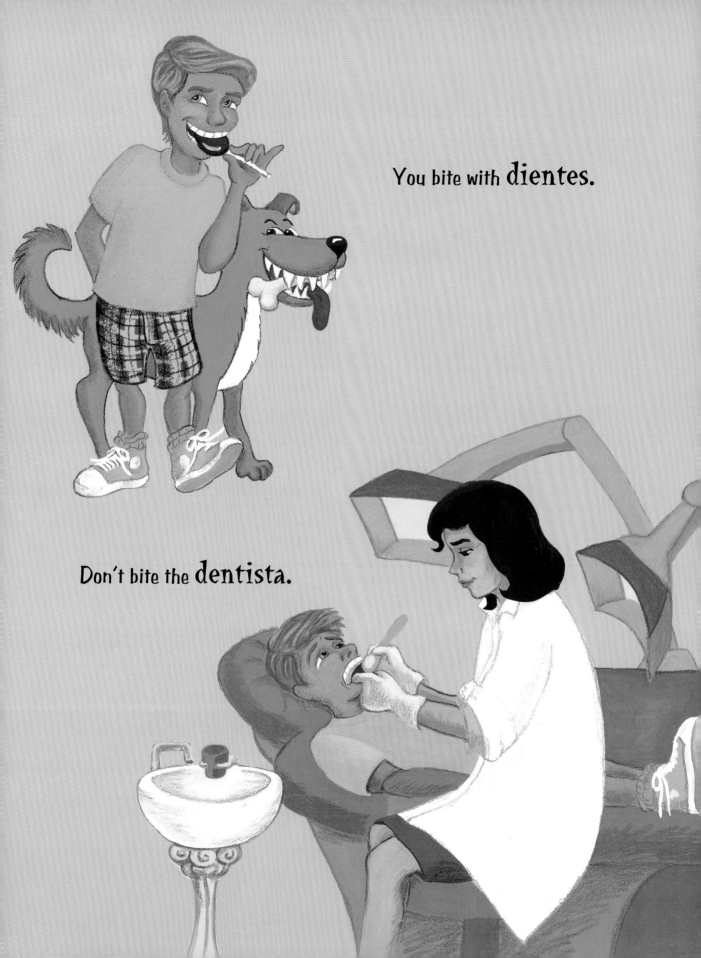

You bite with **dientes**.

Don't bite the **dentista**.

Just wait for your check-up and read a revista.

You study in an **escuela** and dance at a **fiesta.**

Your afternoon nap is called a **siesta.**

A boy is a **niño**,

a girl is a **niña**.

He eats a **pera**,
she eats a **piña**.

Besos are kisses.

Smiles are sonrisas.

Blusas are blouses and shirts are camisas.

Your dad drives a **carro**, same thing as a **coche**.

He drives in the **día** and drives in the **noche**.

Ham is **jamón** and soup is called **sopa**.

You wash with **jabón**

and get dressed in **ropa**.

Wish at a fountain.

Throw coins in the fuente.

Deseos come true. It's no accidente!

A man who makes shoes is **un zapatero.**

Zapatos, or shoes,
cost lots of **dinero.**

The hat on your head is called a **sombrero**.

A cowboy on horseback is called a **vaquero**.

Caliente is hot.

Cold is called frío.

You fish at a lago and raft down a río.

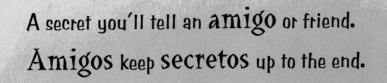

A secret you'll tell an **amigo** or friend.
Amigos keep **secretos** up to the end.

In English and Spanish a burrito's a **burrito**.

A piñata's a **piñata**

and a mosquito's a **mosquito.**

Hola is hello, **adiós** is good-bye.

Spanish is fun, so give it a try!

Glossary

accidente (ahk-see-DEN-teh): accident
adiós (ah-dee-OCE): good-bye
amigos (ah-MEE-goce): friends
árbol (AHR-bol): tree
besos (BEH-soce): kisses
blusas (BLUE-sahs): blouses
burrito (boo-RREE-toe): burrito
caballo (kah-BYE-yoe): horse
café (kah-FEH): coffee
caliente (kah-lee-EN-teh): hot
camisas (kah-MEE-sahs): shirts
carro (KAH-rroe): car
casa (KAH-sah): house
cierra la puerta (see-EH-rrah la PUER-tah): shut the door
coche (KOE-cheh): car
dentista (den-TEE-stah): dentist
deseos (deh-SEH-oce): wishes
día (DEE-ah): day
dientes (dee-EN-tehs): teeth
dinero (din-EH-roe): money
escuela (ehs-KWEH-lah): school
fiesta (fee-EH-stah): party
flor (FLOOR): flower
frío (FREE-oh): cold
fuente (FWEN-teh): fountain
gato (GAH-toe): cat
gris (GREECE): gray
hija (EE-hah): daughter
hijo (EE-hoe): son
hola (OH-lah): hello
huesos (WEH-soce): bones
jabón (hah-BONE): soap
jamón (hah-MONE): ham
lago (LAH-goe): lake
loro (LOE-roe): parrot
madre (MAH-dreh): mother

manos (MAH-noce): hands
mesa (MEH-sah): table
mosquito (moe-SKEE-toe): mosquito
nariz (nah-REECE): nose
niña (NEEN-yah): girl
niño (NEEN-yoe): boy
noche (NOE-cheh): night
ojos (OH-hoce): eyes
padre (PAH-dreh): father
pan (PAHN): bread
parque (PAR-kay): park
pelo (PEH-loe): hair
pera (PEH-rah): pear
perro (PEH-rroe): dog
el piano (el pee-AH-noe): the piano
piña (PEEN-yah): pineapple
piñata (peen-YAH-tah): piñata
plato (PLAH-toe): plate
quesos (KEH-soce): cheeses
revista (rreh-VEE-stah): magazine
río (RREE-oh): river
ropa (RROE-pah): clothing
secretos (seh-CREH-toce): secrets
siesta (see-EH-stah): nap
silla (SEE-yah): chair
sombrero (sohm-BREH-roe): hat
sonrisas (sone-REE-sahs): smiles
sopa (SOE-pah): soup
sorpresa (sor-PREH-sah): surprise
taza (TAH-sah): cup
toro (TOE-roe): bull
vaca (BAH-kah): cow
vaquero (vah-KEH-roe): cowboy
vaso (VAH-soe): glass
zapatos (sah-PAH-toce): shoes
un zapatero (sah-pah-TEH-roe): a shoemaker